MEET THE CARS

Special thanks to: Jay Ward, Phil Lorin, and Geoff Yetter.

Printed in the United States of America

Revised Edition, 2011

10 9 8 7 6 5 4 3 2

ISBN 978-1-4231-4777-0

G942-9090-6-13340

Visit www.disneybooks.com

MEET THE CARS

New York

TABLE OF CONTENTS

INTRODUCTION

Lightning McQueen used to live for the racetrack. But his world has gotten a whole lot bigger. Now he lives in the charming little town of Radiator Springs along Route 66. But his tire tracks are all over the map. Venturing out into Ornament Valley and Carburetor County, he and the gang have met some real characters who live right nearby—including delivery trucks and military vehicles.

And on Friday nights, they even visit the drive-in theater to see some of their favorite actors on the silver screen.

But when Miles Axlerod and the World Grand Prix come knocking, Lightning and his pals start a worldwide adventure, meeting cars from Japan, Italy, and England. From savvy London cabs to fierce sumo wrestlers, their languages, accents, and customs may be different, but they're all pretty similar under the hood, give or take engine construction, transmission fluid, and oh, well, you get the idea. Except maybe for those Lemons. They haven't got a nice bolt in their bodies.

But one thing is universal, whether racing on the tracks of the Piston Cup circuit or on the streets of Europe, race cars all speak the same language—speed. And their fans and staff, as well as the press, just can't get enough.

Seems like it's time to meet some cars. And there's no better place to start than in Radiator Springs. . . .

STAYING CLOSE TO HOME

Out West there's a wonderful little area called Ornament Valley. Whether you're in the town of Radiator Springs or somewhere else in the valley, you'll understand why the cars that live here think there really is no place like home.

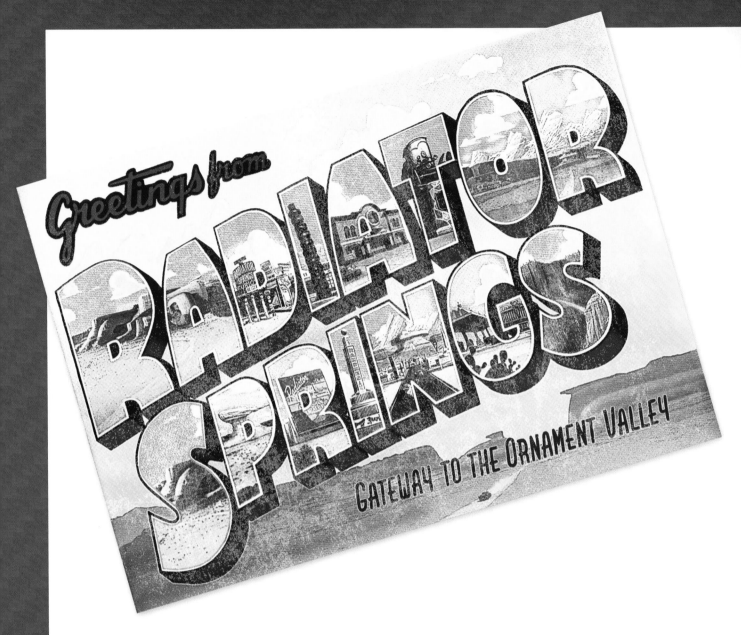

Guidebooks call Radiator Springs "the cutest little town in Carburetor County." Located on historic Route 66, Radiator Springs is a great spot for traveling cars to stop and rest their wheels for a spell. From Flo's V8 Café to Ramone's House of Body Art, Radiator Springs has everything a car could want. And the cars there are the friendliest around. Although the town did face some tough times after it was bypassed by the interstate, the construction of Lightning McQueen's new racing headquarters brought a new wave of excited visitors to the once-forgotten town. Now, Radiator Springs is once again the jewel of Ornament Valley.

When Lizzie rolled into Radiator Springs, it was love at first sight—love for the town itself and for Stanley, the town founder. But she kept Stanley on the soft shoulder for months. Then one day, Lizzie realized that Stanley's vision for a new oasis in the desert had become her dream, too. From that day on, they became the heart and soul of the town—and a couple who were never apart.

VEHICLE TYPE:
1923 Ford Model T 2-Door Sedan

The statue of Stanley marks the very spot where Radiator Springs was founded. As he traveled west, searching for a place to settle and make his fortune, Stanley stumbled upon a natural spring. He stopped to fill his radiator and never left. Soon afterward, Stanley met Lizzie, the love of his life. Together they founded the town of Radiator Springs, which soon became a legendary resting spot for travelers.

VEHICLE TYPE:
McVaporloch Motor Co. Locomobile

MATER

Mater's a good ol' boy with a big heart, and he's the only tow truck in Radiator Springs. Mater runs Tow Mater Towing and Salvage and manages the local impound lot. Though a little rusty, he has the quickest tow rope in Carburetor County and is always the first to lend a helping hand. Mater sees the bright side of any situation, and Radiator Springs wouldn't be the same without him. He doesn't have a mean bolt on his chassis. And when he meets up with some secret agents, he learns he's a natural at undercover work.

VEHICLE TYPE:
Haulital Hook'em

LIGHTNING McQUEEN

Lightning McQueen is an internationally known race car with four Piston Cup wins under his fan belt. He moved to Radiator Springs during his rookie year. The town is home to Team Lightning McQueen's racing headquarters, his closest friends, and his sweetheart, Sally. Built for power and speed, Lightning loves the thrill of a great race. But he's just as happy to slow down for a quiet cruise with good friends.

VEHICLE TYPE:
Handmade, One-of-a-Kind 2006 Race Car

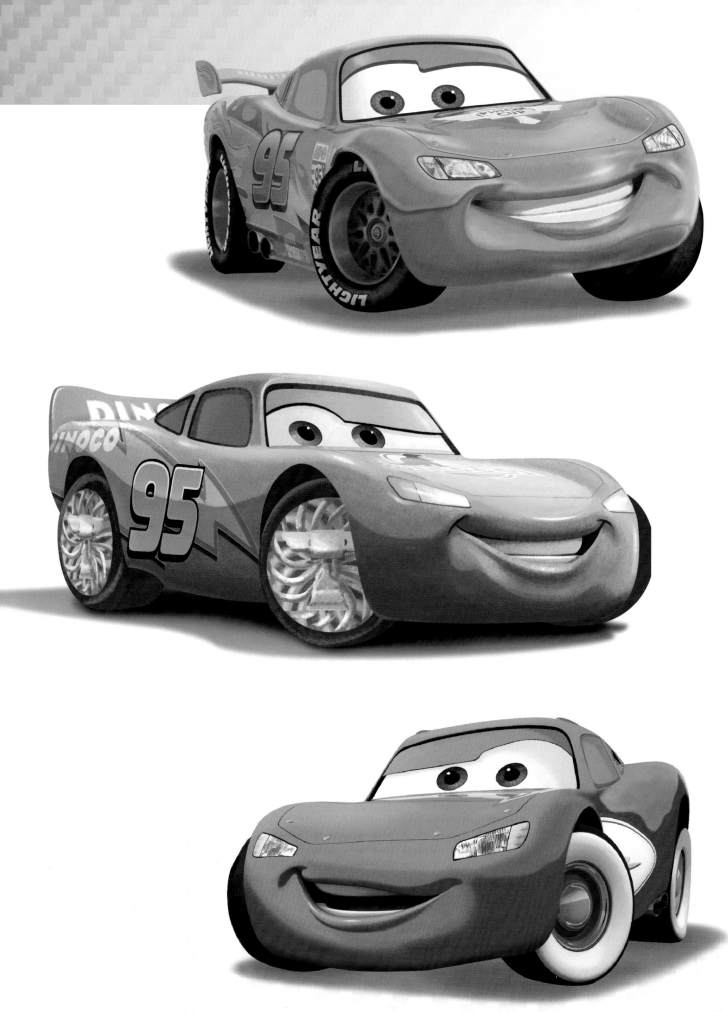

SHERIFF

There's a long history of law enforcement in Sheriff's family. His father was a traffic cop and so were his aunt, his uncle, his two cousins on his mother's side, and his little brother. Even his grandfather was a traffic cop, in New York around the turn of the century. Sheriff always knew he, too, would be a cop. After all, how many other options did he have with a name like Sheriff?

VEHICLE TYPE:
1949 Mercury Police Cruiser

Sally grew tired of her life in the fast lane as a high-powered attorney in Los Angeles, so she made a new start in the small town of Radiator Springs. Charming, intelligent, and witty, she became the town attorney. She also became the car most dedicated to preserving the town's historical beauty. She even bought a motel and restored it to its original condition, and she doesn't plan to stop there. She'd fix the town building by building if that's what it took.

VEHICLE TYPE:
2002 Porsche Carrera

SALLY

DOC HUDSON

Doc Hudson is a car of few words but many talents. He not only serves as the town judge, he's also Radiator Springs' resident doctor. Doc is respected and admired by the townsfolk for the way he looks out for their health and tends to their aches and pains. No one knows too much about Doc's life before he came to town. He keeps his private life private. But if you've got a bad spark plug or a rattle in your engine, his door is always open.

VEHICLE TYPE:
1951 Hudson Hornet

Red may not be a fire truck of many words, but what he doesn't say he shows through his generous actions. Whether it's putting out a tire fire or caring for the beautiful flowers of Radiator Springs, Red is there to support and protect his beloved town. Red takes negative comments about his town very personally. So if you have something bad to say about Radiator Springs, you'd better watch out. Because if there's one thing Red is not afraid of, it's his emotions.

VEHICLE TYPE:
1950s Torchy Truck Co. Fire Truck

Flo first arrived in Radiator Springs as a touring Motorama girl in the 1950s. She was headed west with a group of models when her chaperone had fuel-pump problems just outside of town. Flo and the other show-car girls spent an unforgettable night in Radiator Springs. While she was there, Flo's paint got scratched. But when she went to Ramone for a paint job, he refused to give her one. It wasn't because he was too good to paint her but because she was too good to be painted. When the girls left, Flo stayed. She and Ramone have been together ever since.

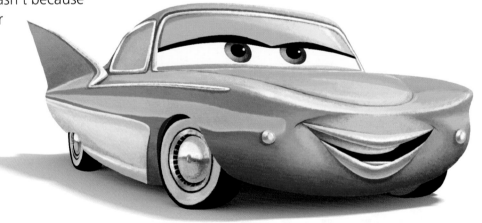

VEHICLE TYPE:
1950s Show Car

RAMONE

A true artist isn't afraid to take chances, to explore new ways to express himself, or to push the limits of culture. Ramone believes that the automotive body can be a vehicle of expression. Every day gives him an opportunity to explore new paint jobs and to push the limitless boundaries of his art.

VEHICLE TYPE:
1959 Chevrolet Impala

SARGE

Sarge loves to tell stories about his daring fearlessness in the military. One time, a tank friend of his lost a belt in the Battle of the Bulge and Sarge towed him to safety. For his bravery, Sarge received the Grille Badge of True Metal! This and medals like it are displayed front and center at Sarge's Surplus Hut, right next to Sarge's very own Mother Road Survival Kit. He guarantees that if you break down, his kit will get you through the night—or the next world war. Even better, it all stows nicely in your trunk.

VEHICLE TYPE:
1942 WWII Willy's Army Jeep

Fillmore is Radiator Springs' resident hippie. A believer in individuality and all things natural, he brews his own organic fuel and preaches about its many benefits. Visitors can try Fillmore's special flavors in the tasting room behind his love-bead and tie-dye-covered geodesic dome. His many conspiracy theories and "naturally" unkempt yard drive his neighbor Sarge absolutely crazy.

VEHICLE TYPE:
1960 Volkswagen Bus

FILLMORE

LUIGI

Luigi runs Luigi's Casa Della Tires, the local tire shop in Radiator Springs. If you're going to drive through this world, why not look good doing it? That's Luigi's motto. Cars may not get to choose their body type, but they all have a choice when it comes to the tires they wear. Luigi offers the finest selection west of the Mississippi. Luigi's Casa Della Tires is known far and wide for impeccable service, competitive prices, and, of course, its very stylish owner.

VEHICLE TYPE:
1959 Fiat 500

Like his boss, Luigi, Guido is a huge Ferrari racing fan. He dreams of being part of a pit crew for a real race car. To better prepare himself, he practices tire changes at night on a wooden frame he built in his garage. One of these days, he hopes to set a new world record for the fastest pit stop of all time. But until that happens, he'll keep trying to learn new things. Currently, Guido is reading *Tire Changes for the Soul* and *Four Tires, One Goal*.

VEHICLE TYPE:
Tutto Forklift

GUIDO

BESSIE

Bessie is Radiator Springs' resident road-paving machine. Everyone agrees she's a low-maintenance gal, but more than one unsuspecting hitcher has learned her quirks the hard way. Doc likes to say laying asphalt with Bessie is more like dancing than paving. Fill her with kerosene, gravel, and tar, and she'll produce the most beautiful ribbon of blacktop you've ever laid rubber on. But you don't want to pull her too fast or get her steamed up. Bessie carries two huge buckets of molten tar and she knows how to use them. Just ask Lightning McQueen!

VEHICLE TYPE:
Basic Service Equipment
Road-Paving Machine

Frank is a hard worker. He spends his days in the fields, harvesting, threshing, and clearing grain. Then it's off to oversee the tractors' work for the rest of the afternoon. By the end of his long day, Frank is ready to power down for the night and prepare for the early morning ahead. So if you're planning to wake Frank, you'd better have a good reason to—or a really good escape route.

VEHICLE TYPE:
XXL MetroActual Combine

FRANK

TRACTOR

Tractors are hard workers. They enjoy what they do, plowing through the fields on a nice day and then falling asleep in the moonlight. But every so often, they wake up to the sounds of snorting and giggling in the distance, and they find themselves lying on their backs staring up at the stars. But they don't mind. It's actually kind of nice to sleep lying down for a change.

VEHICLE TYPE:
Axel Chompers, 4-Cylinder, Diesel-Powered, Easily Frightened Transmission

Dustin Mellows was a delivery truck for Trophy Spark Plugs in the 1950s. The mild-mannered van had a monthly route that took him through Radiator Springs. On one of his regular stops in town, Dustin had a near head-on collision with one of the locals. It all worked out, though. The two cars fell in love and moved to the nearby suburb of Couperville, where they are now enjoying a relaxing retirement together.

VEHICLE TYPE:
Emerycraft Delivery Truck

DUSTIN MELLOWS

ALARM CLOCK

When Sally redid her motel, she wanted every guest who stayed there to wake up with a smile. This original Novelty Clock Car from the 1960s really did the trick.

VEHICLE TYPE:
1960s Novelty Clock Car

Hot on the trail of suspected bank robbers, bounty hunter Timothy Timezone found himself in the sleepy town of Radiator Springs, where he interviewed the locals at Flo's for hours. Ultimately, it was a tip from Luigi that led him to an abandoned silver mine on the outskirts of Carburetor County. There, he single-handedly apprehended the notorious Gasket Gang! It seems the Gasket Gang burned through a lot of tires on their high-speed getaways.

VEHICLE TYPE:
Emerycraft Zinger

TIMOTHY TIMEZONE

GRETA

Greta has decided to get a full-body makeover and a hot new flame job at Ramone's House of Body Art. Tonight she's going to see the renowned body-shop quartet, The Rumbles. The baritone, Chet, is an old traffic-school teacher Greta hasn't seen in years, so she wants to look her best.

VEHICLE TYPE:
Bruchman Salmon Super Sport

Mildred Bylane first passed through Radiator Springs in the 1940s as part of a publicity tour. When she accidentally swerved into a bed of flowers, she found herself rescued by none other than the town's shyest resident—Red. Then Mildred's job called her overseas, but she left Red a single flower to remember her by. To this day, he keeps her memory alive by caring for the descendants of that very flower.

VEHICLE TYPE:
1944 Hollismobile Driftwood

MILDRED BYLANE

VALERIE VEATE

Valerie Veate was a traffic analyst on her way to Portland to start a new job, when she veered off at the Radiator Springs exit to find a place to fill up. Valerie was immediately charmed by the small town. So she offered her services to the city council. Today she is the head of the city expansion committee. She gives advice about how to preserve Radiator Springs' unique historical character.

VEHICLE TYPE:
2002 Cotswell Senator

Nick's secret passion has always been bumper stickers. Fearing the looks he might get from his friends and coworkers, Nick never actually wore any stickers. He just bought them and hid them in his trunk. Then one day, he stumbled upon Lizzie's memorabilia shop. Her bumper stickers were so hilarious that Nick decided it was time to let it all hang out. Now, Nick drives down the road covered bumper to bumper with stickers. He's never felt so free.

VEHICLE TYPE:
Brawny Motor Co.

NICK STICKERS

EDWIN KRANKS

Edwin was a creature of habit: regular oil checks, dinner for one at Flo's every night, and a new coat of tan paint every year. Then, a weekend with some old college buddies led to an unforgettable night. He got a shocking, metal-flake, green paint job. To his horror, no one in town could stop staring at him. But to his surprise, the girls couldn't stop staring, either. Edwin's habits didn't change too much after that, though dinner at Flo's every night became dinner for two.

VEHICLE TYPE:
1944 Piedmont Hauser

Derek "Decals" Dobbs came to Radiator Springs to find work with his old pal Ramone, touching up paint jobs and giving much-needed face-lifts. Derek not only paints cars, he also paints murals. He did a beautiful mural on the side of one of the town shops, declaring Radiator Springs "A Happy Place."

VEHICLE TYPE:
Hollismobile Rumbler

DEREK "DECALS" DOBBS

MILTON CALYPEER

Milton loved cruising around town, greeting and being greeted, as he made his way to nowhere in particular. He worked at the courthouse in Radiator Springs but purposely bought a house at the other end of town, just so he could run into more folks as he made his way to and from work.

VEHICLE TYPE:
Wall-E Motors Sunday Driver 1200

Marilyn has always been very faithful to her stylist, though to be honest, she hasn't been happy with her color for some time now. So, when during a road trip across the country, she and her family stopped off in Radiator Springs, she impulsively stopped into Ramone's body shop, and now she's a stunning purple! Her family loves her new look and so does she, but her stylist back home isn't speaking to her.

VEHICLE TYPE:
ABL Princess

MARILYN

OTIS

Otis is no stranger to the tow hook in Radiator Springs. He's broken down more times than Mater's cousin Betsy after she got left at the altar. He's an old jalopy who wasn't quite up to snuff even when he left the factory, and life's been a challenge ever since. New parts are not available, and he's reached the limit on his roadside service card. In fact, Ramone has repaired him almost weekly for the past few months. Poor Otis just wants to spend some time on the open road . . . trouble free.

VEHICLE TYPE:
1972 Shyster Cremlin

Radiator Springs isn't the only town in Ornament Valley. But eventually the cars who live in the area or are just visiting seem to pass through town, whether it's to go to Sarge's Boot Camp or to get a fresh coat of paint from Ramone. . . .

T.J. comes from a long line of military vehicles, but growing up in the gated communities and private schools of Bloomfield Hills, Michigan, T.J.'s idea of off-roading was going over a pothole on Woodward Avenue. An aspiring rapper, T.J. likes looking tough without scratching his paint or getting dirt on his rims, but all that changed when his father signed him up for Sarge's Boot Camp for Urban SUVs.

VEHICLE TYPE:
Hummer H1

T.J.

LEROY TRAFFIK

Have you ever had one of those days where you get a flat tire, take the wrong ramp onto the freeway and there isn't another exit for miles, and then you desperately need to make a pit stop? Oh, and you're carting a mattress around on your head? Well, this is Leroy, and I guess you could say he's having one of those days.

VEHICLE TYPE:
1992 Hamlet Galavant 1200

For more than sixty years, Miles was known around Ornament Valley as the rain-sleet-or-shine delivery truck. If you needed something shipped fast, Miles was the one to call.

VEHICLE TYPE:
Emerycraft Delivery Truck

MILES

Percy Hanbrakes likes to look good when he goes out on the town. He makes sure he takes a nice, long car wash in the morning. He also makes sure he's got plenty of wiper fluid in case his windshield gets smudged, and he does his best to make sure he's got a touch of that new-car smell. The problem is, by the time he does all that, he tends to forget to check that he has enough gas in his tank.

VEHICLE TYPE:
1944 Emerycraft Towner

Hank used to get into a lot of trouble in his younger years. He'd go drag racing and play chicken with his friends. Hank never lost a chicken race, because he had a problem with depth perception. He couldn't tell that the other cars were getting closer, only that they were getting bigger. He decided it was time to stop goofing around when he lost a curb feeler in a race. That was just a little too close.

VEHICLE TYPE:
Hollismobile Rumbler

HANK "HALLOWEEN" MURPHY

BENNIE CALIPER

Bennie Caliper loves movies. He goes to the theater every chance he gets, and he loves the way a good story can take you away from all the day-to-day troubles of your life. He is currently working on his first original screenplay about a cop car that's forced to partner up with an inner-city garbage truck. It's called *Trash Talkin' Cop.*

VEHICLE TYPE:
Remirunabout Menv

Swift Alternetter had dreams of being a heavyweight champion. He could pull a rig four times his own size! But he never followed that dream because being a heavyweight rig-pulling champion involves a lot of traveling, and Swift, well, he doesn't like to fly.

VEHICLE TYPE:
Remirunabout

SWIFT ALTERNETTER

Duff has a lot of steam to blow off, especially considering that he's a diesel. He spends most of his time working out at the gym, pulling rigs, and practicing tough-guy comebacks to himself in the mirror. But when faced with actual conflict, he's as shy as a four-cylinder.

VEHICLE TYPE:
2000 Equalizer Mule

Bertha Butterswagon has made a mint off her custom line of license-plate frames, each one hand painted with little teddy cars. They've swept the nation and can be found in auto-parts stores everywhere. Who knew a homemade holiday gift for her sister would become such a hit?

VEHICLE TYPE:
Remirunabout Menv

BERTHA
BUTTERSWAGON

AT THE THEATER

For a bit of Friday night fun, there's no better place to go than the drive-in movie theater—unless it involves tipping tractors, of course. These cars have starred in some of the top movies of all time. But they're not just movie cars—they've got lives of their own, too.

PT FLEA

Circus promoter PT Flea has spent his life motoring around backyards, literally looking under every rock to find the next big act, such as the "Screaming Wheelies." Their tires squealed so loudly every headlight in the audience shattered. PT is still paying off the insurance bills on that one.

VEHICLE TYPE:
Nimbly Co., No-see-um LX

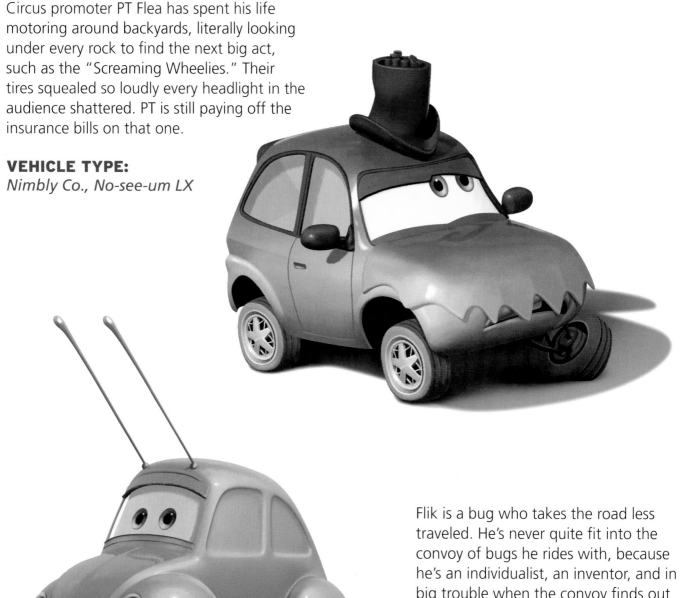

Flik is a bug who takes the road less traveled. He's never quite fit into the convoy of bugs he rides with, because he's an individualist, an inventor, and in big trouble when the convoy finds out that the warrior vehicles he's hired to save them are actually circus cars.

VEHICLE TYPE:
Special Aphid GT

MIKE

Mike is the top Scare Assistant at Monster Trucks, Incorporated. He assists his best friend and number one all-time Scarer, Sulley. Mike is a wise-crackin' guy who loves joking around more than he loves working, but together the two make a great team.

VEHICLE TYPE:
Heebie-Jeebie Buggy Inc. Cycoupe

Sulley is the top Scarer at Monster Trucks, Incorporated. He's looked up to by all the other trucks in the Scare Garage because he's the biggest, baddest, blue-ist thing on four gigantic wheels. But deep down inside, he's as gentle as a hybrid.

VEHICLE TYPE:
Scream Motors

SULLEY

YETI

The roads are pretty bad in the Himalayas, so it's a good thing Yeti can plow through even the highest snowdrifts. Always on the lookout for stranded motorists, Yeti doesn't just help dig them out of the snow, he also likes to offer a delicious snow cone or two while they wait.

VEHICLE TYPE:
*Behemoth Corp.
Abominable Snowplow*

Hamm is the slyest piggy bank on wheels. This ceramic armored car has an explanation for everything, though it may not always be the correct one. Hamm is the watch car for Andy's Garage, keeping an eye on the flow of traffic to see who's coming and who's going.

VEHICLE TYPE:
Porkster Baconbit

HAMM

WOODY

Woody Toy Car may have been pushing the miles and a little over his warranty, but he was still a favorite in Andy's Garage. Until one day a new model rolled off the assembly line—a high-tech, low IQ oil slick named Buzz Light Car. Suddenly Buzz has a prime parking spot in Andy's Garage and Woody's parked on the street.

VEHICLE TYPE:
Toy Car

Buzz Light Car has crash-landed in a place called Andy's Garage. Desperate to reunite with the rest of the Space Rangers, he enlists help from the native vehicles of this strange planet. But before he can get his ship fixed, Buzz is confronted with the shocking realization that he may not be the Space Ranger Lunar Rover he always thought he was—but rather nothing more than a toy space car.

VEHICLE TYPE:
Toy Car

BUZZ

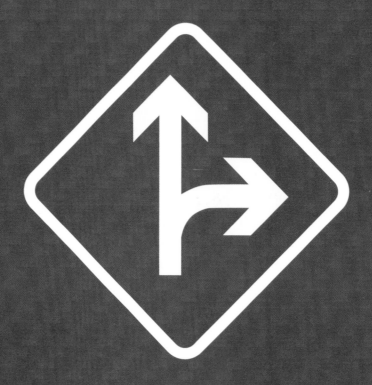

MOVING ALONG

Whether you're on an interstate or a back road in Italy, adventure is around every corner. The great thing is that no matter where you go, you'll meet all kinds of new cars, and maybe even a train or a plane.

ON THE ROAD

If you need to get somewhere fast, there's no better way than the interstate. With wide lanes and smooth tarmac, this type of road is built for speed. However, if you prefer to slow down and take in the scenery, roads like Route 66 are the ones for you. Adventuresome tourists, long-haul truckers, and tricked-out imports are just some of the folks you may meet along the way.

Mini and her husband, Van, love to get out and see the world. Unfortunately, they rarely see their exit. Getting lost on vacation has become somewhat of a tradition for the couple. Mini enjoys the unplanned detours. They allow her to see interesting places and folks that she would never have planned on visiting. She just wishes Van could enjoy that time to stop and smell the roses—and if not, then at least stop and ask for directions.

VEHICLE TYPE:
Chauncey Motors 200 HP 3.8-Liter V6

Van and his wife, Mini, love to travel: the only problem is they don't know where they're going. The two share a strong sense of adventure, but unfortunately, a stronger lack of direction. This turns most of their relaxing getaways into strenuous marathons over mountainous terrain, through the desert, and past every gas station—as Van would rather stall then ask for directions.

VEHICLE TYPE:
Chauncey Motors 170 HP 3.3-Liter V6

VAN

OLIVER LIGHTLOAD

Oliver pretends to be a long-haul trucker, but the truth is he just likes the Top Down Truck Stop. You see, he's actually an online stockbroker and lives less than a mile down the road. He likes to pop in at the truck stop once in a while to crack some jokes, take a nap, or just listen to stories from the truckers who go through on their way to someplace far-off and exotic.

VEHICLE TYPE:
Luxoliner Semi-Hauler

Ben considers the open road his home, fellow truckers his family, and the Top Down Truck Stop his dining room. He has few close buddies but makes friends in every town he passes through. Once Ben has met somebody, he never forgets their name. He can recognize a familiar grille anywhere.

VEHICLE TYPE:
Northernstar Semi-Hauler

BEN CRANKLESHAFT

GIL

Industrial waste recycling might be a messy gig for some, but no load is too big or too toxic for Gil. But it's the jokes Gil tells at the truck stop that he enjoys recycling most of all. The other trucks politely nod and chuckle as Gil tells the same old one-liners time and time again.

VEHICLE TYPE:
Peterbilt Semi-Hauler

Jerry's a pretty easygoing guy. Nothing makes him happier than running routes on the open road. There's no one to report to, no need to wash every day. It's the best! There's only one thing that can put him in a bad mood, and that's being mistaken for a Mack truck. After all, he's a Peterbilt and proud of it!

VEHICLE TYPE:
Peterbilt Semi-Hauler

JERRY RECYCLED BATTERIES

DJ

From an early age DJ, whose full name is Devon Montgomery Johnston III, was interested in all kinds of music. He had a voracious appetite for collecting records and was a gifted student at a nationally renowned East Coast music conservatory. One evening at a friend's party, Devon met a gentleman by the name of Wingo. An expert in paint and body modification, Wingo designed a custom paint job for Devon and a wicked sound system to match. Now going by the name DJ, Devon revels in his treble but never loses touch with his bass!

VEHICLE TYPE:
Reko-do Spinner

Boost wasn't always a gang leader. When he was younger he worked at a garage for elderly cars where he befriended an early drop-tank racer who turned him on to the ways of racing with Nitrous. Learning from the master, who had racked up records on the Great Salt Lake, Boost promised the old-timer he'd keep the tradition alive.

VEHICLE TYPE:
Kyoku Jitsu

BOOST

SNOT ROD

Snot Rod took his doctor's advice and headed west to find some clean, crisp mountain air to relieve his chronic allergies. On the way, he met up with Boost, DJ, and Wingo! The highly modified car group made him the head of security and crowd control. He still has allergies and explosive sneezing attacks, but his ability to clear the road of pesky traffic is unmatched and much appreciated by his buddies—who like the road all to themselves.

VEHICLE TYPE:
Bragatron

In grade school, Wingo's outrageous, inappropriate paint schemes didn't comply with the school's strict paint code and got him into big trouble. These days, Wingo makes a good living designing paint schemes for an illustrious clientele at his own custom-paint shop. Now that his paint jobs don't get him into trouble, Wingo and his gang find new ways to do that.

VEHICLE TYPE:
Wingo

WINGO

Everyone's road is a little different. Sometimes, it's even in the sky or on the rails. And cars are always glad to meet new folks—even if they don't roll the same way.

Crabby is a Seattle-based crab boat, made gruff by years spent crabbing in the turbulent Bering Sea. With Norwegian fuel powering his engine, the white hulled, dark blue-trimmed vessel is officially registered as the Northwestern, though his colleagues and competitors just call him Crabby. He's 103 feet from bow to stern and is usually packed to the hilt with crab pots.

VEHICLE TYPE:
1977 FV Northwestern

CRABBY

EVERETT

Everett is the first jumbo jet in a long line of passenger jets, with each generation of his family getting a little longer and wider. But Everett doesn't mind. After all, when you're racking up close to two million frequent-flier miles and hauling cars back and forth across the Pacific, size is synonymous with a smooth, comfortable flight—and that's what Everett is known for. That, and taxiing too fast. There's nothing like the feeling of eighteen squishy tires landing on the tarmac.

VEHICLE TYPE:
2008 Jumbo Jet

Daniella used to work as a waitress at the Flaps Down Fly & Drive-in near her small town's airport, and for hours she'd watch the planes land and take off. Fascinated by travel, Daniella got to know the local planes during their layovers. She was always courteous and brought them refreshments. One day, something dawned on Daniella—she could do her job up in the air! The next day she signed up to be a Turboloft flight attendant.

VEHICLE TYPE:
2009 Servi-kraft

DANIELLA MUFFLER

MEI AND SATSUKI

Mei and Satsuki are not identical twins, so don't even ask. Both are sweet and delightful and make it a point to remember your first name when they check you in at the first-class lounge desk. A word to the wise: if you're trying to slip into the lounge without credentials, you'd better go through Mei, the younger one. She's way more lenient.

VEHICLE TYPE:
2009 Microlux 4000

GALLOPING GEARGRINDER

The Galloping Geargrinder has been riding the rails of Carburetor County since the 1930s. The Geargrinder was light on the tracks and extra efficient at running the mail into little towns like Radiator Springs. But by the 1950s, the delivery work dried up as the semitrucks began using the new straight-line highway that bypassed the old, curving train route. Other Geargrinders ended up at amusement parks and tourist traps, but old GG prefers to continue chugging along on his original line—and to keep Mater from trespassing in the tunnels!

VEHICLE TYPE:
1935 Rio Grande GG

Stephenson is a state-of-the-art bullet train. On paper, he runs twice daily, from Kent to London, but in reality he's a British high-speed spy train, who scrambles switchboards, hops international rail lines, and can make it from Dover to Porto Corsa in five hours. He has no dining car and no spare compartment because he's filled with the finest in high-tech, classified spy gear and probably has a few secret agents aboard. So don't bother waiting for him at the station. . . .

VEHICLE TYPE:
2005 VFT KL-2

STEPHENSON

WELCOME TO JAPAN!

The first race of the World Grand Prix is held in Tokyo, and while the gang is there, they also get a taste of the culture—from meeting sumo wrestlers to feasting on sushi with wasabi.

ZEN MASTER

A master in the art of sculpting sand in the serene Zen rock garden at a Tokyo museum, Zen Master wears his old, woven reed hat and uses his antique wooden rake to create mesmerizing patterns.

VEHICLE TYPE:
Piaggio Ape

As a professional sumo wrestler at an arena in Tokyo, Kingpin Nobunaga is a gold-painted microvan who fights his fiercest matches when he's wearing his lucky purple *mawashi*.

VEHICLE TYPE:
2004 Yoko Zuna XL

KINGPIN NOBUNAGA

PINION TANAKA

Pinion Tanaka is a gold-painted micro van and a professional sumo wrestler from Tokyo who's always a menacing sight in the ring in his signature teal *mawashi*.

VEHICLE TYPE:
2004 Yoko Zuna XL

Kimura is an accomplished calligrapher and one of the most precisely tuned SUVs you'll ever meet. It's rumored that he has never made an incorrect call in a sumo match—just another reason why the Japan Sumo Association is lucky to have Kimura-san as one of their top-ranked *gyoji* referees. He keeps the fight rolling along, calls a wrestler in or out-of-bounds, and when his *gunbai* war fan points, the winner has been chosen. No questions asked.

VEHICLE TYPE:
2005 Shonosuke Matchfair G

KIMURA KAIZO

OKUNI

Okuni is a microcar Kabuki dancer who dons the traditional white-painted face and an exquisite, colorful kimono for her performances at Kabuki theaters in Tokyo.

VEHICLE TYPE:
2009 Microlux 4000

Taia used to be an ordinary, gray truck in the muffler transport business, working the Sawara-to-Tokyo line. But he dreamed of more exciting things than peddling parts, so he moved to Tokyo to get into advertising. Now, painted a shiny yellow and purple, with stainless trim and two gigantic TV screens, Taia certainly attracts attention. In fact, he's the most popular truck in town—he can turn any boring party into a drive-in movie with the flip of a switch!

VEHICLE TYPE:
2003 Terebi T-Star 1000

TAIA DECOTURA

HALLO, LONDON!

From Petroldilly Circus to Big Bentley, London
is filled with history. It's really an ideal place to
visit, especially if you can swing being knighted,
like Sir Tow Mater.

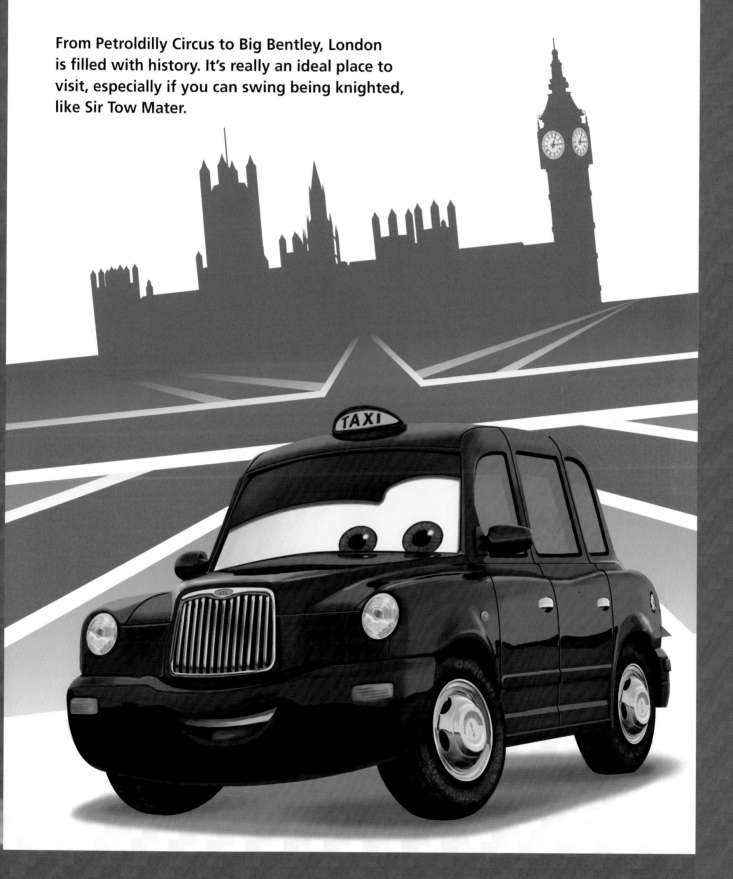

THE QUEEN

With the final stage of the World Grand Prix taking place in the historic streets of London, England, The Queen is quietly elated about being invited to preside over the finish line by Sir Miles Axlerod. Painted in the most royal shades of blue and never without her jeweled crown, The Queen is the definition of decorum and regality. But that doesn't mean she doesn't enjoy a bit of first-rate competition!

VEHICLE TYPE:
1953 Royalcraft Mark II

PRINCE WHEELIAM

Prince Wheeliam of England is an avid racing fan. He can't believe his luck that the final race of the one-of-a-kind World Grand Prix is happening on the streets of London. Though he must remain impartial when by his grandmother The Queen's side, he is privately rooting for his fellow Brits Lewis Hamilton and Nigel Gearsley to cross the finish line first.

VEHICLE TYPE:
2009 Bentley Continental

Sgt. Highgear is a member of the regiment assigned to London's landmark Buckingham Palace. With the recognizable tall bearskin cap atop his scarlet body, he stands guard at his sentry box with pride and conviction.

VEHICLE TYPE:
1962 Land Rover Series IIA

SGT. HIGHGEAR

TOPPER DECKINGTON III

Topper Deckington III is a classic British double-decker bus in a vivid shade of red, who relishes his daily Killswitch route through London's famous bustling Petroldilly Circus.

VEHICLE TYPE:
1968 Roadruler Bus

No one knows the sites, streets, or shortcuts of London better than the jovial Chauncy Fares, a quintessential London cab.

VEHICLE TYPE:
2004 LTI TXII Taxi

CHAUNCY FARES

CIAO, ITALIA!

Luigi and Guido hail from Italy, and so it feels a little like home when they visit for the World Grand Prix with Lightning and the rest of the gang, who find the area *bellissimo*!

UNCLE TOPOLINO

In the small village of Santa Ruotina near Porto Corsa, Italy, Luigi's favorite uncle, Topolino, lives with his beloved wife, Mama Topolino. Uncle Topolino is the owner of the village's tire shop, where he taught Luigi and Guido everything they know, though Uncle Topolino is full of sage advice about more than just tires.

VEHICLE TYPE:
1937 Fiat Topolino

To all who know her, Luigi's aunt, Mama Topolino, is a masterful cook with the best fuel in the village of Santa Ruotina. She has a loving but fiery relationship with her husband, Uncle Topolino, and she shows her love and generosity for both family and friends by feeding everyone her renowned *delizioso* fuel.

VEHICLE TYPE:
1951 Bella Machina Model B

MAMA TOPOLINO

CARLO MASERATI

Carlo Maserati is one car you can't judge by his buttoned-up appearance. The eldest of seven cars, Carlo engineered his own performance modifications at a very young age. Off he went, speeding into new adventures and power-sliding out of them. His only other passions were the love of fast, curvy cars and the finest olive motor oil. You'd never know it by looking at him, because on the surface he looks street legal and civilized, but under the hood there's enough horsepower to throttle you.

VEHICLE TYPE:
2006 Maserati Quattroporte

MAMA BERNOULLI

As the mother of Italy's winningest race car, Mama Bernoulli couldn't be prouder of her son, Francesco. As a former Grand Prix star herself, she taught him everything he knows. She used to attend every one of Francesco's races, but her motor can't take the oil pressure anymore. Every time a race begins, she shuts her windshield and whispers to *Il Gran Produttore* ("the Great Manufacturer") to keep her little Francesco safe and, of course, to let him win!

VEHICLE TYPE:
1961 Formula MB1

Sal is about as gentle and old-world as they come. A busy little bee, he scoots around, up the steep hills of the Tuscan town of Carsoli, Italy, with his sweet-smelling exhaust trailing behind. More than making up for his small size by being an ape-of-all-trades, Sal can be found hard at work on any given day. But most evenings he's at the local café, sipping regional olio with his *amici*, and bidding passing microcars, "*Buona sera.*"

VEHICLE TYPE:
1967 Piaggio Ape

SAL MACHIANI

UNCOVERING SECRET PLOTS

Sometimes a day at the races is more than just a
day at the races. When bad things are afoot, you
want the best secret agents on the case.

SECRET AGENTS

In the world of international espionage, these cars are elite agents, trained to get the job done right—and with flair. Equipped with the latest in spy gadgetry, these secret agents can call on high-tech tools to help them foil any evil scheme.

LELAND TURBO

Leland Turbo, British Intelligence. He and Finn McMissile go way, way back together in the world of espionage, and they even trained together in the academy as new recruits. They were partners early in their careers and owe each other their lives, getting one another out of tough spots many, many times. Clearly, Leland is not one to run from danger. In fact, he thrives on it . . . but this time it may end up costing him more than he thinks.

VEHICLE TYPE:
1965 Runwell Type SR

Siddeley is a state-of-the-art British twin-engine spy jet. At 176 feet from nose to tail and with an impressive 157-foot wingspan, the supersleek, silver-bodied Siddeley streaks through international skies at record-breaking speeds. Outfitted with all the latest in high-tech spy equipment, including cloaking technology, defensive weaponry, and afterburners, Siddeley is Finn's steadfast partner in fighting crime around the globe.

VEHICLE TYPE:
2004 Glidesworth A113

SIDDELEY

FINN McMISSILE

Finn McMissile is a master British spy. Though charming and eloquent, it's his stealth maneuvering, intelligence, and years in the field that enable him to thwart unexpected attacks from bad guys and make daredevil escapes. Finn's design is sleek and timeless, but he's also prepared for any tricky situation with an arsenal of ultracool gadgets and weaponry, including front and rear grappling hooks, a missile launcher, deployable magnetic explosives, and a holographic disguise emitter.

VEHICLE TYPE:
1965 Faultless GT

HOLLEY SHIFTWELL

Holley Shiftwell is a beautiful young British desk agent turned spy-in-training. Well-educated and sharp, she knows every trick in the book—or rather, she relies on every trick in the spy manual. She's armed with the latest state-of-the-art spy equipment imaginable, from hidden cameras and concealed weapons to a telescoping utility arm and a holographic pop-up display. Holley is a highly motivated agent, but she is fresh out of the academy, so her experience is based on lessons learned in school rather than in real-life situations. But it didn't take too long before she learned to wing it.

VEHICLE TYPE:
2008 MT-R Mark II

ROD "TORQUE" REDLINE

Rod "Torque" Redline is considered by many to be the greatest American spy in the world. Recruited after the Cold War for both his brains and brawn, Torque is a tough-as-nails Detroit muscle car with a mastery of disguises. In his most recent deep-cover operation, he obtained vital information about the plot to sabotage the World Grand Prix. So Rod planned a rendezvous with his British counterparts so he could share share his discoveries at the World Grand Prix welcome reception in Tokyo, Japan. But the bad guys were hot on his tailpipe, so Rod was forced to ditch the intel early with the first party guest he saw—a rusty American tow truck named Mater.

VEHICLE TYPE:
2006 Deringer DXR

Tombér is a dubious little French car with an unusual, and very unstable, three-wheeled design that befits the meaning of his name–to fall. By trade, he deals car parts from a stall in a Parisian market—though his questionable merchandise sources have led to his reluctant acquaintance with British secret agent Finn McMissile.

VEHICLE TYPE:
1968 Cargatti Trois

TOMBÉR

BAD GUYS

Jalopies, rust buckets, clunkers. For too long, the Lemons have been mocked for their odd designs and unreliable engines. Now, the Lemons want power and the respect that comes with it. To achieve their goal, they want to discredit Sir Miles Axlerod's new alternative fuel, forcing cars to buy oil from the Lemons. They're willing to destroy any car that parks in their way. And let's not forget the masterminds behind their plot. . . .

Being stuck on an oil rig for 90-day shifts, Muggsy found himself watching a lot of old movies. He absolutely loves film noir and has been known to reenact scenes from his favorite crime thrillers. He lifted the name Muggsy to give himself more deep-sea cred, but who's he kidding. He's a harmless rig worker. When Professor Z comes on deck to address his minions, Muggsy knows it's time to snap back into forklift mode and get lifting.

VEHICLE TYPE:
2006 Liftloader

MUGGSY LIFTSOME

MILES AXLEROD

Sir Miles Axlerod is a former oil baron who seems to have sold off his fortune, converted himself into an electric vehicle, and devoted his life to finding the renewable, clean-burning energy source of the future. Once he developed his wonderfuel Allinol, he created the World Grand Prix to show it off. But don't be fooled by Axlerod's shiny coat of paint! Deep down, his heart is as black as his fuel filter. As secret leader of the Lemons, Axlerod is ready to destroy any car that tries to stop him.

VEHICLE TYPE:
1978 Branford Axlerod

Professor Z is an intelligent, manipulative mad German scientist who uses his talents for evil. A sophisticated weapons designer, he has constructed a device that can harm—even kill—cars from great distances without leaving a trace. His handiwork is used to sabotage various racers participating in the World Grand Prix, a multinational race that features the world's top athletes, including Lightning McQueen.

VEHICLE TYPE:
1958 Kleinwagen 250

PROFESSOR Z

GREM

Grem is a dented, rusty-orange AMC Gremlin. After years of being dismissed for his design, even being called a "Lemon," Grem has a big chip on his fender, and it has led him to the underworld of international espionage. As a henchman for his villainous boss, Professor Z, Grem and his partner-in-crime Acer are trying to sabotage the World Grand Prix and the famous race cars competing in it. When Grem and Acer mistake Mater for an American agent with important top secret information, the ruthless Lemons set out on a round-the-globe chase to stop Mater from foiling their evil scheme.

VEHICLE TYPE:
1975 AMC Gremlin

Acer had always felt like an outcast in the car world, so the beat-up green AMC Pacer joined forces with the Lemons. As henchmen for the devious Professor Z, their clandestine mission is to wreak havoc at the highly visible World Grand Prix. Acer must hunt down the American and British secret agents who've stolen crucial information about Professor Z's underhanded plot. His primary target just happens to be Mater, who has been mistaken for a spy. Acer tries very hard to be a tough guy, but he's over-eager compared to his no-nonsense accomplice, Grem.

VEHICLE TYPE:
1974 AMC Pacer

ACER

J. CURBY GREMLIN

J. Curby is the current patriarch of the Gremlin crime family, but he got there by some unconventional roads. Don't let the rough exterior fool you—he was once maître d' at the flagship restaurant of superstar chef Motorio Brake-tali. He even soaked in the best of the big city's shows. These days, J. Curby has turned to a life of mischief, serving up danger and singing a more ominous tune . . . .

VEHICLE TYPE:
1975 AMC Gremlin

While other boys in school had cool racing stripes, Tyler Gremlin was stuck with hockey-stick stripes, and they were cheap decals to boot. Picked on in school for his goofy graphics and lack of horsepower, it came as no shock that his personality got a bit menacing as time went on. The mischievous Tyler would drive without his headlights on after dark, or chain a police officer's chassis to a lamppost. He became so salty that if any car so much as tooted their horn they would get T-boned. Most cars learned to yield to him. If a car tried to stand up to him, they'd have to hit-and-run because he always came back swinging . . . just like a hockey stick.

VEHICLE TYPE:
1975 AMC Gremlin

TYLER GREMLIN

PETROV TRUNKOV

Petrov hails from a tiny village on the Baltic Sea, where temperatures in winter drop down to a frigid -10°C. And if that's not enough, the salty air and rocky roadways have irreversibly corroded his body panels. But Petrov really doesn't mind. In fact, he likes his engine air very cool and thinks the bubbling rust makes him look more "mileage mature." Add that to the fact that he carries most of his weight in his rear end and it's a wonder he doesn't break in half when the going gets rough.

VEHICLE TYPE:

1973 Avto Trunkov T-73

Before becoming the leader of the Trunkov family, Vladimir was a gray-market parts smuggler behind the "Iron Bumper." But when the power in his country shifted back to an autocracy, he changed his name and went underground. Known on the street as "Big Ears" because of two side-panel air inlets, Vladimir was able to hear trouble coming kilometers before anyone else. With so many close calls, Vladimir doesn't know how many strokes he's got left in his engine.

VEHICLE TYPE:
1971 Avto Trunkov T-71

VLADIMIR TRUNKOV

TUBBS PACER

Tubbs never set out to lead a crime family; it just worked out that way. As a Pacer in the car world, you don't get much respect just on your looks, so you have to earn it. That's why he embraced his negative nickname, Upside-down Bathtub, and dubbed himself Tubbs. Before long, he was running with a pack of other disrespected Pacers who were also tired of being called jelly beans and junkers. They met up with Professor Z and a whole new bushel of Lemons looking for the same car-world credibility. Tubbs proved his loyalty to this new family over and over, and he soon found himself poised to help take over the world.

VEHICLE TYPE:
1974 AMC Pacer

Fred misses his early days growing up in Kenosha. Back then, he didn't have to worry about being the toughest Lemon on the block, or where he would get his spare parts. All he had to think about was kicking back and relaxing with fellow Pacers and Gremlins. As time went on, the factory parts dried up in his hometown, and Fred had to look for new adventures in faraway places. That led him to sign up for work on a mysterious oil rig in the deep Pacific. As long as the pay is steady and the parts don't dry up, Fred's not complaining.

VEHICLE TYPE:
1974 AMC Pacer

FRED PACER

VICTOR H.

The dreaded Victor H. is the head of the Hugo crime family. Sure he's known to break down quite often, has leaky seals and gaskets, and is still waiting on major replacement parts to get him back on the road again, but "Mr. H" has got Karl to haul him and Ivan to tow him wherever he needs to go. Now that he's the leader of an entire crime organization, Victor has the other Lemons shaking in their tires, and he runs the syndicate like the well-oiled machine that he's not!

VEHICLE TYPE:
1983 Volgar Hugo NG-1

Karl has one job: to take Victor H. wherever he wants to go. A luxury transporter for the rich and villainous, Karl keeps his privacy glass up and his eyes on the road, and he doesn't ask too many questions. Sure, he misses the simpler days of moving legitimate business cars to and from garages, but hauling the main crime boss is just too lucrative for him to even think about getting out now.

VEHICLE TYPE:
2007 Porteur Chauffeur VH

KARL HAULZEMOFF

ALEXANDER HUGO

Alexander Hugo is not who you think he is. He is also known as Chop Shop Alex and Alexander the Not–So–Great, among other names. He's got a rap sheet a mile long and connections to the Hugo organized crime family. He's currently wanted in France, Germany, the Czech Republic, and Serbia, so check his rap sheet before you go anywhere with him.

VEHICLE TYPE:
1984 Volgar Hugo NG-1

Most tow trucks just look tough, but Ivan really is tough. From his front grille to his rear hook, he's built solid. What else would you expect from Victor H.'s personal chauffeur? The rumor that he demolished a subcompact with one drop of the tow boom may sound preposterous, but it's absolutely true. Still, every tough truck has a weakness, and for Ivan it's helping a pretty sports car with a flat tire. All she has to do is give a wink and a shy smile, and he's ready with "roadside assistance."

VEHICLE TYPE:
1983 Hookov H9

IVAN

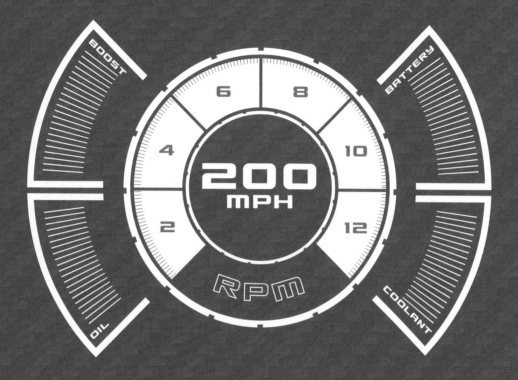

START YOUR ENGINES

There's just nothing like a good race to get your engine running. Lightning McQueen rules the Piston Cup Circuit. But then he has to see if he can take a brand-new championship by traveling to Japan, Italy, and England in the World Grand Prix.

PISTON CUP CIRCUIT

Don't blink or you'll miss these speedy racers. Each car has his or her own strategy for getting ahead on the racetrack, but they're all angling for the same thing—the Piston Cup! To win, a racer needs to place first at the challenging Dinoco 400. Held every year at a different speedway, the Dinoco 400 is the biggest event in American racing. And no car can win it alone; every racer needs a great pit crew and a supportive sponsor if they want to take home the coveted trophy.

TEAM RUST-EZE

Rust-eze might not be the most glamorous sponsor
in racing, but they have the fastest car on the circuit.
Rust-eze owners Rusty and Dusty gave Lightning
McQueen his start in racing. Now Lightning is a
four-time winner of the Piston Cup, and he shares
that honor with his fantastic team.

MACK

Mack spends endless days and sleepless nights crisscrossing the country. For some, this life would quickly grow old. But not for Mack. He knows how important his role is. He drives for Lightning McQueen, the world's fastest race car. He's part of the team, and everyone knows there's no "I" in team, just like there's no "I" in Mack.

VEHICLE TYPE:
Mack Semi-Hauler

His name is not Chuck, not Chucky, not Chuckmeister, not Chaz, not Chet, not Charlie, and not Charles. He's a firm believer that a racer is only as good as his tires are fresh, so his motto is, "Change them early and change them often."

VEHICLE TYPE:
2003 Nemomatic Propane-Powered Forklift

NOT CHUCK

DUSTY RUST-EZE

Dusty and his brother, Rusty, like to help out their fellow rusty cars almost as much as they like telling jokes. That is why they invented Rust-eze Medicated Bumper Ointment. Whether it's some browning around the wheel well or a bumper that's completely falling off, Rusty and Dusty are there with a can of Rust-eze to fix it, or at least ease the burning, itching, and soreness that plague so many cars.

VEHICLE TYPE:
1967 Dodge A100 Van

Rusty and his brother, Dusty, created a small empire working out of their mother's garage in Boston. It's been over fifteen years, and their mother has watched their operation grow into a household name, with factories all over the country. Rusty and Dusty's mother says she couldn't be prouder of her two boys' accomplishments, but she hopes that their next big move will be out of her garage.

VEHICLE TYPE:
1963 Dodge Dart

RUSTY RUST-EZE

TEAM DINOCO

Team Dinoco represents the most sought-after sponsorship in the circuit. And they have certainly earned that distinction. Seven-time Piston Cup champ The King leads his team with an old-fashioned dedication to hard work and fair play.

STRIP "THE KING" WEATHERS

From his humble beginnings on the Piston Cup circuit to the glitzy sponsorship and media attention he has today, Strip Weathers (also known as The King) has seen it all. This seven-time Piston Cup champion is the winningest race car in all of Piston Cup history. He's loved every second of his racing career, but, truth be told, The King is ready for a slower pace. He's looking forward to more time with his queen, Mrs. The King.

VEHICLE TYPE:
1970 Plymouth Superbird

Luke was The King's very first pit-crew member. The King's pit stops may have taken a lot longer with only one pitty, but everything was done better. For years now, Luke has been having dinner at The King's house every Tuesday night, and their wives are in a bowling league together.

VEHICLE TYPE:
Nemomatic Propane-Powered Forklift

LUKE PETTLEWORK

GRAY

Gray always knew that because of his size he'd be hauling cargo across the country—gas, lumber, maybe even steel, like his dad. But he never dreamed that his cargo would be seven-time Piston Cup champion, Strip "The King" Weathers.

VEHICLE TYPE:
Luxoliner Semi-Hauler

Tex has been Dinoco's team owner and talent scout for more than twenty years. Sure, he's a smooth talker from the Lone Star State, but he's also a genuine guy with a big heart. He knows it takes more than flash and big talk to win—it takes loyalty, smarts, and a lot of hard work. And Tex ought to know; he started Dinoco with just one tiny oil well. Now he runs the largest oil empire in the world.

VEHICLE TYPE:
1975 Cadillac Coupe de Ville

TEX

DINOCO GIRLS

Those nine blue-feathered beauties on deck at the Dinoco publicity tent are the "Dinocuties." They're the last dancers standing after a fierce competition in which the gals lived in a giant dorm and competed on television. On the final episode, Strip "The King" Weathers picked the winners.

VEHICLE TYPE:
Various Axxelo Models

A high-performance executive helicopter, Rotor Turbosky is ready at a moment's notice to take The King wherever he needs to go. He provides a faster and smoother ride than those small whirlybirds, and he's a proud card-carrying member of Team Dinoco.

VEHICLE TYPE:
Whirlybird Liftalot High-Performance Executive Helicopter

ROTOR TURBOSKY

TEAM CHICK HICKS

Team Chick Hicks is willing to do whatever it takes to win, even if that means cheating its way to the top. If you're in between Chick and the finish line, watch out! This team always has a dirty trick in mind.

Chick Hicks is a racing veteran with a chip on his shoulder. He has cheated his way into more second-place finishes than any other car. He's been counting down the seasons to The King's retirement so that he can take over the coveted Dinoco sponsorship. He never expected such fierce competition from hotshot race car Lightning McQueen.

VEHICLE TYPE:
1979 Shyster Cremlin

CHICK HICKS

CHICK'S CREW CHIEF

Chick's loyal crew chief has been the number one guy to the second-place race car for over ten years—through the good, the bad, and the ugly. He longs for the day when Chick will win a Piston Cup so that he will no longer be the second-best crew chief on the racing circuit.

VEHICLE TYPE:
200½ Ton Truck 5.7 L V-8

Bruiser Bukowski has been a part of Chick's pit crew for ten long years. Before that, they were in high school together, and before that they were in drama club together. Bruiser is Chick's number two fan, only because the number one spot was already taken by Chick himself.

VEHICLE TYPE:
Shystermatic with a Mustache Hookup

BRUISER BUKOWSKI

MORE PISTON CUP RACERS

Lightning McQueen, The King, and Chick Hicks may be the leaders of the Piston Cup, but they're not the only racers on the circuit. Watch these guys try to give Lightning a run for his money.

CHUCK ARMSTRONG

Chuck has always had a slight allergy to certain fuels. The side effects make it not so pleasant for other cars to be within five feet of him. Once he started racing professionally, not only did the problem not go away, it actually got worse due to the high speeds. It got so bad the other cars didn't want to pass him. Chuck hopes he's a good example for taking a problem and turning it into something good.

VEHICLE TYPE:
Axxelo Fission

Rusty Cornfuel grew up on a farm in Mississippi. He ran a racing circuit there with his buddies. Rusty won most of the races and almost made enough profit from the events to sponsor himself professionally. Luckily, a sponsor came along. Now Rusty can spend his own money on more important things, like flying his buddies from the farm to every race.

VEHICLE TYPE:
Brawny Motor Co. Spark GT

RUSTY CORNFUEL

RUBY "EASY" OAKS

Nicknamed Easy for his laid-back attitude, gravelly voice, and slow way of talking, Ruby Oaks's view of life mirrors his approach to racing. He likes to take it easy, gather his thoughts, get folks to let their guard down, and then when they least expect it, take the lead.

VEHICLE TYPE:
Crown Celesta

Todd Marcus is known as the best race car ever from Dieselton, Alabama. He's also known as the only race car to come from Dieselton, Alabama. When asked why he chose to be car number 123, he simply replied, "Because it's easy to remember." And that's why it's also his ATM number, his Internet log-in, his home security code, and his safe combination.

VEHICLE TYPE:
Axxelo Fission

TODD "THE SHOCKSTER" MARCUS

RALPH CARLOW

Number 117, Ralph Carlow, is the little brother of famous Hollywood actor Jordon Carlow. The two brothers once had little respect for what the other did for a living, but when Jordon got a movie role playing a race car, he was forced by the studio to spend time shadowing his brother, Ralph. After two long months of research, Jordon came away with a new respect for how hard racing really is. And after seeing his brother's performance in the film, Ralph gained a new respect for acting. Now Jordon never misses a race, and Ralph never misses a premiere.

VEHICLE TYPE:
Brawny Motor Co. Spark GT

Misti Motorkrass comes from a racing family, but not a racetrack family. Her brother Frank is a champion street racer. Her brother Zach holds the title as the fastest drag racer in three towns, and legend has it that her brother Dave has outrun five police cars in the past year alone. Misti's family is very excited about her career. Though she may not have the perfect track record, at least it's clean!

VEHICLE TYPE:
Crown Celesta

MISTI MOTORKRASS

Lee practiced driving on the family farm. He recalls an old, rickety bridge over a river where he'd try to "thread the needle across that narrow bridge." Lee credits his nerves of steel to those daredevil runs. These days, Lee threads through Piston Cup traffic every Sunday, competing with some of the fastest cars in the world!

VEHICLE TYPE:
Axxelo Fission

Floyd Mulvihill originally trained as an automotive engineer. One day, he decided to put down his tools and pursue his lifelong passion to race. He competed in the Junior Piston Cup pro series with the likes of Sage VanDerSpin and graduated to the Piston Cup in 2005. He's affectionately known as "Smokey Floyd" because he enjoys laying long patches of burning rubber in front of adoring fans.

VEHICLE TYPE:
Stodgey Suaver EX

FLOYD MULVIHILL

MURRAY CLUTCHBURN

Murray Clutchburn's first taste of competition was as a member of the 1984 gold-winning Auto Games test-track relay team. You might recognize him from specially marked boxes of Wheelies Shredded Brakes! After the Auto Games, he went straight into mainstream professional racing. Now he has a flourishing career in the Piston Cup series.

VEHICLE TYPE:
Stodgey Suaver EX

Johnny Blamer is simply one of those cars other racers love to crash into. He's been involved in more collisions than any other car in Piston Cup history, earning him the nickname Magnet Face. He's also known as the hardest working car on the circuit, though he hasn't finished a race in the ten years he's been competing. He holds the record at 545 starts and zero finishes.

VEHICLE TYPE:
Capitol Motors

JOHNNY BLAMER

KEVIN RACINGTIRE

With little natural athletic ability, knowledge of racing's rich history, or understanding of its complex rules, it's a wonder Kevin Racingtire has been able to last in the Piston Cup circuit for as long as he has. He says his success is because of his family, particularly his father-in-law, who is the owner of the large pharmaceutical company that just so happens to sponsor the team for which he races.

VEHICLE TYPE:
Capitol Motors

Billy Oilchanger's dream is to become a racing color commentator after he retires. He's watched the greats over the years, and even practices announcing by calling the races out loud to himself while he's in them. It's great experience, though the other drivers find it distracting and even a little creepy.

VEHICLE TYPE:
Sherpa Motors Iota GT

BILLY OILCHANGER

RYAN SHIELDS

Ryan is not only the View Zeen Corrective Windshields driver, he's also a customer. Without View Zeen, the race is merely a blur of multicolored blobs moving at two hundred miles per hour. His windshield doesn't just help out on the track, it also has a special coating that helps cut down on glare while driving at night, not to mention it makes him look smarter.

VEHICLE TYPE:
Crown Celesta

Kevin is the fourth in a long line of racers in the Shiftright family. His great–grandfather Kurt raced on the old dirt tracks of the 1950s. Kevin's grandpa Kraig won two Piston Cups in the late 1970s and his dad, Klint, won three in the early 1990s. Kevin tries not to let the pressure of his family history get to him when he's on the track—or at the dinner table.

VEHICLE TYPE:
Axxelo Fission

KEVIN SHIFTRIGHT

DIRKSON D'AGOSTINO

Dirkson D'Agostino discovered his natural racing talent while working in a graphics department for a small racing outfit. Running errands between buildings, he'd dodge all kinds of obstacles at insane speeds. One day, Dirkson caught the eye of the racing shop's owner, who fired the young upstart for what he considered reckless driving in the workplace. Then he rehired him as one of his pro racers. He could tell Dirkson had a natural talent for the track.

VEHICLE TYPE:
Capitol Motors

Slider Petrolski's parents named him Slider after his uncle, famed dirt-track racer Slide Powers, who graced the gritty, makeshift tracks of the late 1940s. Slider wanted to be like his uncle. He started racing at an early age. He challenged postal trucks, taxis, and delivery vans, as well as all varieties of unsuspecting pedestrian motorists. He even raced a police car, but only once.

VEHICLE TYPE:
Capitol Motors

SLIDER PETROLSKI

SAGE VanDerSpin

Youngest winner of the Junior Piston Cup Pro Series, Sage VanDerSpin entered the Piston Cup competition in 2004 already a highly decorated racer. His favorite trackside activity is dodgeball. Several other racers play with him as well, but it's the pitties who are the toughest competition on the court, says VanDerSpin, because they're tiny and have arms.

VEHICLE TYPE:
Brawny Motor Co. Spark GT

Greg loves his sponsorship, but there is one aspect he's not a fan of: the paint job. Gingerbread brown with candy-cane lettering would likely not have been the first choice of a professional graphic designer, but it was, however, the first choice of the owner's four-year-old niece. Greg also doesn't really enjoy judging the annual contest in which fans build a likeness of him out of real gingerbread and gumdrops.

VEHICLE TYPE:
Capitol Motors

GREG "CANDYMAN"

DARREN LEADFOOT

Darren Leadfoot is the LAST guy you want drafting you on the final turn. Known for suddenly speeding up at the end of the race, Darren is one car who won't let anything—or anyone— stand between him and the finish line!

VEHICLE TYPE:
Axxelo Fission

European racer Haul Inngas came to the United States in the early 1990s. Because he won so many races on some of Europe's most challenging tracks, when he arrived in the US, lots of team owners wanted to sponsor him. However, one night Inngas accidentally drove on the wrong side of the road coming home from a bowling alley! Luckily, his ego was the only thing seriously damaged. He returned to win the Piston Cup championship later that year.

VEHICLE TYPE:
Brawny Motor Co. Spark GT

HAUL INNGAS

BRUSH CURBER

Brush Curber is considered to be one of the most consistent veteran Piston Cup contenders. Curber had numerous top-ten finishes in the 2006 season, but a string of midseason malfunctions sidetracked his run for the cup. With help from his Fiber Fuel sponsor and an overhauled diet, Brush changed his losing ways. He also thinks his recent success was helped by his loving wife of forty years, Katherine, and their fourteen children: Hal, Brush Jr., Penelope, Jake, Marty, Willard, Ingrid, Lucille, Scotty, Wendell, Aimee, Kassidy, Florence, and Truman.

VEHICLE TYPE:
Sherpa Motors Iota GT

An Ivy League school may seem like an unlikely place to get started in the racing world. Only a couple of years ago, Winford Bradford Rutherford was grille-deep in physics books, learning about momentum, velocity, and anything else that would give him an edge on the track. His doctor and lawyer friends at the country club thought he was crazy, but the studying paid off. Winford is now a highly respected Piston Cup racer. He uses his vast knowledge of physics to cheat the wind and outmaneuver his fellow racers, who affectionately call him "The Professor."

VEHICLE TYPE:
Capitol Motors

WINFORD BRADFORD RUTHERFORD

RACE STAFF

Running a world-famous race requires the best cars in the business. And so does being part of a pit crew. These cars keep the Piston Cup races running smoothly so the racers can focus on winning, instead of on rowdy fans or bad track conditions.

A former National Guard rapid-deployment specialist, Chief No Stall takes no chances with his crew's safety! Known as the toughest crew chief on the circuit, he barks out orders so loudly that No Stall race car Todd Marcus swears he can hear the chief's directions on the track with or without a radio.

VEHICLE TYPE:
Haulital Lugnutter

CHIEF NO STALL

PETROL PULASKI

Petrol Pulaski used to ride with the Eighth Street Carburetors until police vehicles picked him up after a downtown street brawl. Since being placed in a rehab program that eventually led him to his first assignment trackside, Petrol has become a role model for ex-gang forklifts everywhere.

VEHICLE TYPE:
2003 Nemomatic Propane-Powered Forklift

Stacy works for Leakless Adult Drip Pans. She's a propane-powered forklift who likes living in the city and listening to country. She's no Guido, but she's pretty quick with a tire change!

VEHICLE TYPE:
2003 Nemomatic Forklift

STACY

JERRY DRIVECHAIN

Jerry trained for years to be a stunt car but never quite made the cut. It certainly wasn't for a lack of talent, though. The truth is, forklifts just don't make good stunt cars. Thankfully, Jerry could always fall back on his legendary juggling abilities. If you're lucky, you'll spot him practicing in the wee hours of the morning in various secluded parking lots.

VEHICLE TYPE:
2003 Nemomatic Forklift

Brian thought it would be fun to sell antenna balls at the racetrack for a summer—the problem is, that summer was ten years ago. He had hoped to start seriously pursuing his singing career in September, but one thing led to another and his part-time job became his career. But Brian does enjoy the excitement of the racetrack, and sometimes when he's calling out, "Get your antenna balls here!" over the roaring crowds, he likes to imagine he's belting out a classic show tune over the cheers of his adoring fans.

VEHICLE TYPE:
P-150 Courier 4-liter V6

BRIAN PARK MOTORS

TOW

As the official tow rig of the Piston Cup circuit, Tow has pulled his share of battered, weepy champions off the track. He's seen the top racers in their lowest moments, but he always respects their privacy.

VEHICLE TYPE:
Houslital Crew Cab

Tom is a Piston Cup race official, but that doesn't mean he's not a fun guy. Sure, rules and regulations are important to him, but he also enjoys a good joke or a fun prank now and then. He once switched the signs on entrance C-44 of the stadium with C-45 to temporarily confuse his fellow race officials. The prank worked like gangbusters and everyone had a good laugh . . . except Tom, who felt guilty and reported the incident to his superior.

VEHICLE TYPE:
Remirunabout Orbit

TOM

As a youngster, Dex dreamed of being a real racer. But a four-cylinder compact pickup isn't exactly designed for the racetrack. Dex found a way to put himself in the middle of his favorite sport, though. He climbed the ranks from selling pennant flags in the stands to becoming top flagman on the circuit. His caution-flag pattern is a thing of beauty. If it weren't for Dex, the races would never start—and they'd never end either.

VEHICLE TYPE:
Pabloloco 4-Cylinder Compact Pickup

Charlie Checker is the Piston Cup's official pace car. Charlie wears his amber lights with pride. He's not what you'd call a horsepower champ, but he doesn't mind. After all, he's always in the lead, and NOBODY passes him. That's exactly how he likes it.

VEHICLE TYPE:
Capitol Motors 2004 Econ

CHARLIE CHECKER

MARLON "CLUTCHES" McKAY

When you're cornered by a mob of ferocious paparazzi, there's no one better to call than Marlon "Clutches" McKay. A veteran whose time was spent largely as an armored troop carrier, he traded in his bulletproof glass to pursue his dream of becoming a Motor Speedway of the South security team leader. He loves nothing better than locking grilles with nosy camera sidecars and personally showing them the exit.

VEHICLE TYPE:
Capitol Motors 2004 Econ

Never mess with Marco Axelbender. This former ATF pursuit vehicle received a presidential commendation when he blew out three tires during a high-speed pursuit, yet he still managed to catch the assailant on nothing but rims. Today, he treads safer roads at the Los Angeles International Speedway, arresting scalpers and turning away the riffraff.

VEHICLE TYPE:
Emerycraft Inka

MARCO AXELBENDER

AL OFT

Al is high on life. As an enormous billboard in the sky for the Lightyear Tire Company (proud sponsor of the Piston Cup), he loves to provide those grand images from high above the track. And he's very happy that his job sends him to great sporting events, because he always has the best view in the house.

VEHICLE TYPE:
Lightyear Blimp

Barney Stormin is a professional skywriter. His job not only requires aerobatic skill and relatively low winds, but most importantly, good spelling. Because, as Barney likes to say, "There is no eraser in the sky."

VEHICLE TYPE:
Wacool Biplane Co.

BARNEY STORMIN

WORLD GRAND PRIX RACERS

To promote his new fuel, Allinol, Sir Miles Axlerod created the World Grand Prix. Consisting of three races, one in Japan, one in Italy, and one in England, the World Grand Prix is the ultimate showcase for the globe's greatest racing talent. Each course has a unique mix of classic straightaways, technical turns, and track types, meaning racers have to be masters of several racing styles if they want to stay competitive. But only one car can be WGP Champion. . . .

FRANCESCO BERNOULLI

Francesco Bernoulli grew up in the shadow of the famous Monza racecourse in Italy where he and his friends would sneak onto the track and race the famous Pista di Alta Velocita bank turn. He was an instant winner on the amateur circuit and soon became an international Formula racer champion. The ladies love Francesco's open wheels, youngsters admire his winning spirit, and fellow racers envy his speed. But Francesco's biggest fan is Francesco himself, as evidenced by his racing number. As the most famous race car in Europe, #1 Francesco is Lightning McQueen's chief rival in the World Grand Prix.

VEHICLE TYPE:
*2009 Formula FB1
Prototype Racer*

World Grand Prix contender Carla Veloso hails from Rio de Janeiro, Brazil. The sweet but powerful Latin diva can dance the night away at "Car-nival," but she spends most of her time on the racetrack. After setting a new track record at the local Interlagos circuit, she was drafted to join the 24-hour endurance racing team in Europe, where she posted a consistent series of podium finishes. In the World Grand Prix, the proud Brazilian Le Motor Prototype racer is the only female in the field, and Carla is ready to prove to the world that #8 is there to win for her home country.

VEHICLE TYPE:
2009 Le Motor Prototype B12 Racer

CARLA VELOSO

NIGEL GEARSLEY

Nigel Gearsley, from Warwickshire, England, is an Aston Martin DBR9 racer bearing #9. He got his start racing the Speed Hill Climb—a unique, completely uphill race through the Aston Hill mountain area that his family has run for generations. Nigel's racing career has been anything but an uphill challenge, as he's won nearly every start in the past few years on the Grand Touring Sports Car circuit, including a string of podiums at Nürburgring and Le Mans. His cool British refinement makes him an imposing presence on the World Grand Prix courses.

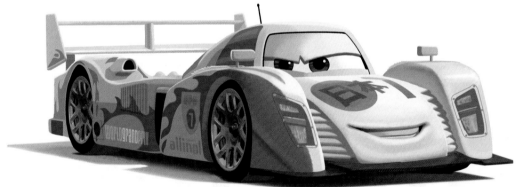

VEHICLE TYPE:
2008 Aston Martin DBR9 Racer

Shu Todoroki is a Le Motor Prototype racer representing Japan and bearing #7 in the World Grand Prix. Shu was raised at the base of the active Mount Asama volcano in Japan and soon became a champion on the Suzuka circuit. His sleek design sports a fiery red Ka-Riu dragon, which Shu borrowed from Japanese legend because he relates to its quiet, yet fierce nature. His team legacy is filled with victories—his coach was the only Japanese car to ever win at Le Mans—and Shu hopes to prove that he is a champion-level racer on the international stage of the World Grand Prix.

VEHICLE TYPE:
*2006 Le Motor
Prototype J8 Racer*

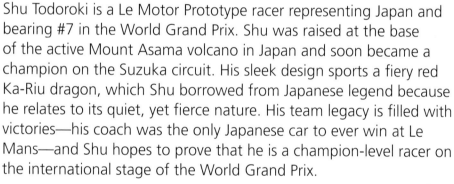

SHU TODOROKI

JEFF GORVETTE

Jeff Gorvette is one of the greatest race cars alive today. His ability to succeed on the big ovals as well as on the road courses has made him respected around the world. Having moved from his hometown of Vallejo, California, to Indiana to be closer to the racing world, Gorvette's ability to succeed at all levels at such a young age has turned hoods wherever he competes. His "Rookie of the Year" awards and number of top ten finishes are unmatched.

VEHICLE TYPE:
2009 Corvette C6.R

Max Schnell started as a humble production sedan from Stuttgart. An avid amateur racer, Max would practice alone on the back roads of the dense Black Forest—a trek that one day caught the eye of a racing team owner. Soon Max was on a professional circuit, and as his horsepower increased, he converted himself to carbon fiber, dropping his weight and getting into prime racing shape. He's won more races at Motorheimring than any other World Touring Champion League car in history. A naturally brilliant engineer, he used logic and analytics to refine his build, making him a perfectly calibrated race car.

VEHICLE TYPE:
2009 World Torque League Championship Racer

MAX SCHNELL

MIGUEL CAMINO

Spain's most famous, admired, and lusted over car is Pamplona's Miguel Camino. The GT2 caught the eye of the entire country while participating in the Running of the Bulldozers—initially, he was just a fan, but he soon found himself in the ring with the dozers. His flair, style, and speed as a *toreador* inspired a generation of young bulldozer fighters, and soon, that same speed and flair turned heads on the racing circuit. Open and funny, Miguel is the life of any party.

VEHICLE TYPE:
*2007 Grand Touring
Sports SS-E Racer*

Known as the "World's Greatest Rally Car," #6 Raoul ÇaRoule was born in Alsace, France. A restless soul, Raoul joined the famous Cirque du Voiture French circus where he studied *gymkhana*—a graceful, drift-filled motor sport that taught him pinpoint timing and an unparalleled ability to navigate tricky courses with ease. He's the first car to ever win nine consecutive rallies. Raoul is confident he can use his rally experience to pull ahead of his fellow World Grand Prix racers during the three courses' touchy dirt sections, especially with his fans waving banners that read: ÇaROULE Ca-RULES!

VEHICLE TYPE:
2006 Global Rally Car Racer

RAOUL ÇaROULE

LEWIS HAMILTON

Lewis Hamilton, the famously sleek and seriously fast #2 Grand Touring Sports champion, has been a determined and winning racer for most of his young life. Like all youngster cars, Lewis spent his childhood going to school, taking karate lessons, and winning the British Karting championship by the age of ten. Today, he continues to bring an exceptional work ethic and soft-spoken confidence to the racecourse, where his extraordinary achievements speak for themselves via a spotless track record on the junior and professional circuits. His car carries the flag of Grenada, home to his family, who immigrated to Britain in the 1950s. His unrivaled technical skills, natural speed, and cool, karate-inspired attitude make him a powerful contender.

VEHICLE TYPE:
2009 Grand Touring Sports Special GBG Racer

The former European colony and newly independent Republic of New Rearendia is desperate to put its name on the map, and the #10 open-wheeled racer Rip Clutchgoneski is the country's best bet. After putting together a remarkable string of qualifying races, Rip's entry into the World Grand Prix is clearly the Cinderella story of the competition. Though Rip credits luck for his chance on the international stage, skill and exuberance are what really brought the proud New Rearendian racer to the starting line.

VEHICLE TYPE:
2005 Formula 6000 Racer

RIP CLUTCHGONESKI

WGP CREW CHIEFS

While the racers are giving it all they've got on the course, the crew chiefs are always working behind the scenes to get their team an extra advantage. Strategy is key to winning the World Grand Prix, and these chiefs are the world's best.

GIUSEPPE MOTOROSI

Giuseppe may have "*la dolce vita*" now, but back in the late 1960s, he had a major spill on the "Curva Parabolica" at Monza during a big race. Thankfully for us, his previous accident couldn't steer him away from the motor-sports world entirely, and he never lost his passion for winning. Signor Motorosi quit racing and has now partnered with fellow Italian and Formula Race champion Francesco Bernoulli. He is confident that they'll sweep the series at the WGP, and if there's one car who knows Francesco better than he knows himself, it's Giuseppe.

VEHICLE TYPE:
1967 Alfa Romeo Duetto 1600 Spider

You'd think being born and raised in tropical Brazil would make Cruz Besouro the most laid-back crew chief at the WGP. Not true. Although air-cooled, that hasn't stopped Cruz from being one intense little Beetle. He's been known to put 100 kilometers on his odometer in one race just by pacing back and forth while he barks instructions in the pits. On the other hand, his driver, Carla Veloso, is pretty used to it, and she always responds with a level head. Cruz may be aggressive, but his technical knowledge of racing makes him the best chief Brazil's ever known! *Pra Caramba!*

VEHICLE TYPE:
1960 Volkswagen Beetle

CRUZ BESOURO

Austin may weigh a lot less than a ton, but boy does he pack a punch! Coming from a long line of miniature champions, he used to be one of England's premier rally racers. Austin's power-to-weight ratio fooled many competitors into underestimating him, leading to a string of British championships and a long-term role as a crew chief. His reputation for racing success was key in Nigel Gearsley's request to be coached by Austin at the World Grand Prix. With Austin's underdog nature and Nigel's renowned skill on the track, this pair is hard to beat.

VEHICLE TYPE:
1961 BMW Mini Cooper

Otto dabbled in sports-car racing early in his career, as many WTLC racers come from his family, but he found his true calling as a team crew chief. His technical prowess, eye for meticulous detail, and laserlike focus led Max Schnell to partner with Herr Bonn early in his racing career. The winning pair has racked up a number of Torque League cups around Europe, and they're now poised to take their rightful place in the World Grand Prix.

VEHICLE TYPE:
1998 Audi TT Coupe

PETRO CARTALINA

Petro is an unassuming little coupe, but don't let the mild-mannered appearance fool you. He's a Corsa for a reason. Racing is in his oil lines, and he knows how to analyze racing circuits to find the quickest path to victory. From the moment he saw his long-time racer Miguel Camino take the checkered flag at Circuit de Car-talunya, Petro knew that they had a shot at taking the World Grand Prix by storm.

VEHICLE TYPE:
2009 Opel Corsa

Don't let his tough-guy name fool you, Bruno is really a softie. He plays the accordion, likes romantic drives along the Seine, and his favorite movie is *The Engine of Dr. Motoreau*. But just because he's cultured doesn't mean he can't race. He comes from a long line of French rally racers, and his hydraulic suspension has helped him rise above many difficult situations, both on and off the track. This ability to handle all terrains in any situation led him to Raoul ÇaRoule, and the pair is rallying for victory at the World Grand Prix!

VEHICLE TYPE:
1974 Citroen DS23

BRUNO MOTOREAU

MACH MATSUO

Mach used to be one of the world's most successful production sports-car racers. He found winning success on the sands of Baja, in European rallies, and in sports-car club races around Japan. When Mach got the offer to be a LeMotor crew chief, he realized it was time to start training and shaping Shu Todoroki into a World Grand Prix champion!

VEHICLE TYPE:
1970 Nissan Fairlady Z

Bruce is among the world's most demanding crew chiefs. He's notorious around the racing world for his intense, revved-up training sessions. Bruce is incredibly strict on his current racing champion, Lewis Hamilton, keeping him on a daily regimen of 100 hot laps and 2 hours of chicane work each morning. He expects Hamilton to maintain the same technical discipline, whether he's casually driving around town or going all-out in competition. With focused training like this, it's no wonder that Boxmann and Lewis are a highly favored team to win at the World Grand Prix.

VEHICLE TYPE:
2005 ABG P4700

BRUCE BOXMANN

JOHN LASSETIRE

John is a legendary crew chief, having extensive team experience in both the Piston Cup and the American Grand Touring Sports racing classes. Known for a cool head under stress, decisive leadership, and the ability to get the job done, John has that golden clutch. All these skills led to his being paired with his longtime friend in racing, Jeff Gorvette. Now the winning pair is gearing up to take it all at the World Grand Prix.

VEHICLE TYPE:
Classic Luxomatic JL-57

MEET THE PRESS

Who's always there to cover the latest racing news? Who's at the track even earlier than the racers, hoping to get a juicy scoop? Who knows every detail about all the top racers? The press cars! Whether they're at the stadium for a Piston Cup race or covering a road race for the World Grand Prix, they give viewers at home the inside story on all the latest drama both on and off the track. Although a few press cars are willing to stretch the truth to sell a story, most reporters know that racing is exciting enough without adding their own details.

DARRELL CARTRIP

D.C. is a Southern gentleman and ex-Piston Cup champion, and he knows what it takes to win. He's in the booth with Bob Cutlass for every major Cup event, calling the play-by-play and adding humor and personality to the commentary. But when the racing flag drops, he's all business. That is, until he shouts his signature, "Boogity, boogity, boogity! Let's go racing, boys!"

VEHICLE TYPE:
1977 Monte Carlo

Bob Cutlass is a world-renowned sports announcer. He's covered every sporting event from tractor pulls to monster-truck rallies, including the last three Auto Games, but he's most famous for teaming up with former Piston Cup racer Darrell Cartrip to announce Piston Cup racing on the Racing Sports Network. Bob Cutlass is the voice of reason to Darrell's enthusiastic and colorful commentary.

VEHICLE TYPE:
*1998 Saxon GTSC Grand
Touring Sport Coupe GHi*

BOB CUTLASS

KORI TURBOWITZ

The smoky-voiced Kori Turbowitz started her career as a voice-mail operator. But her delivery of "You have . . . THREE new messages" was spoken with such flair and irreverence that the next thing she knew, she was the number one morning-show host on the radio in the Bay Area as well as one of the top Piston Cup reporters on television.

VEHICLE TYPE:
2005 Luxomobile Animatic

Chuck Manifold started out in the news business as Barry Pipenloo. But when he started covering the racing scene, he knew that he needed a name better suited for the tough nature of the circuit. As soon as he started reporting as Chuck Manifold, his career took off faster than a drag racer at a green light.

VEHICLE TYPE:
Capitol Motors

CHUCK MANIFOLD

SKIP RICTER

Skip Ricter has been reporting about the racing scene for years. After doing volunteer radio broadcasts of race-day action in college, he got an internship at a local television station. He soon made his mark with the launch of his weekly race recap entitled *The Race Machine*, which can now be seen in twenty-three cities.

VEHICLE TYPE:
Brawny Motor Co. Shindig SR

Integrity. That's the first rule for any decent member of the press. Tim Rimmer is not a decent member of the press, though. He's a tabloid photographer for a local supermarket rag. But even Tim wouldn't give Chick Hicks the satisfaction of having his photo taken while he celebrated his "stolen" Piston Cup win.

VEHICLE TYPE:
Axxelo

TIM RIMMER

CHUCK "CHOKE" CABLES

Chuck Cables hails from the Midwest but somehow found himself in California, covering the biggest race of the season! A live telecaster for twenty years with the Plainville Pavement Press, he recently made the jump to RSN (Racing Sports Network) and became one of the hottest not-so-minivan cams on the news team!

VEHICLE TYPE:
Pabloloco Lugnutter

Houser Boon was the first photographer to coin the now-famous phrase "Show us the bolt!" He called it out at a press event, and Lightning McQueen actually turned right toward him and flashed his million-dollar lightning bolt. It was indeed a proud moment for Mr. Boon—if he'd only trademarked the phrase, he could have retired twenty years earlier.

VEHICLE TYPE:
Crown Celesta

HOUSER BOON

RON HOVER

During the week, Ron Hover is a news chopper for CRSN, but when he's not covering a big race, he's covering a big fire with thousands of gallons of water. Ron is a volunteer firefighter in Sonoma County. A thrill-seeker by nature, Ron loves the excitement of his work and enjoys helping out his community.

VEHICLE TYPE:
Whirlybird Liftalot

Dan Sclarkenberg knows news. And knowing news like Dan knows news allows Dan to cruise for new news that might not be known. Naturally, knowing news as soon as Dan knows news puts him in the know, and since he knew it when it was new and is thus able to report it in the now, then yes, Dan knows news.

VEHICLE TYPE:
Park Motors Perk EX

DAN SCLARKENBERG

BERT

Someday, when Bert finds a gallery that understands his abstract motion-blur photography, he will finally be recognized as the true artist that he is. In the meantime, though, it's his job as a paparazzo that pays the bills. And yes, paparazzo is the singular of paparazzi. And yes, it means "oversized mosquito" in Italian.

VEHICLE TYPE:
Ducham Futuro

Cora Copper is one of those news hounds you never want to tangle with—especially if you've got something to hide! A tireless (some say ruthless) investigator, she's uncovered dirt on the cleanest circuit racers—anything that will sell copies of her paper, *AutoVan Empire*!

VEHICLE TYPE:
Axxelo Rapido SI

CORA COPPER

BRENT MUSTANGBURGER

Brent Mustangburger is an American sports broadcasting icon. With the self-proclaimed "best stall in the garage," the excitable 1964½ Ford Mustang is widely considered one of the most recognizable voices in the history of automobile sports television and is associated with some of the most memorable moments in modern sports. At the World Grand Prix, Brent will be calling the turn-by-turn action with informed analysis and unparalleled zeal.

VEHICLE TYPE:
1964½ Ford Mustang

Originally from Royal Leamington Spa, England, David Hobbscap is a worldwide racing luminary. His 30-year career in professional racing spans the globe as well as all types of motor sports. Now David shares that priceless knowledge as a race announcer who is well known for providing comic relief during broadcasts. A former champion with 20 starts at 24 Hours of Le Mans, his storytelling comes from personal experience. Anything but your ordinary television sportscaster, David can't wait to enlighten and entertain the World Grand Prix audiences.

VEHICLE TYPE:
1963 Jaguar E-Type Lightweight Racer

DAVID HOBBSCAP

RACING'S BIGGEST FANS

Every racer loves the roar of the crowd. But some fans go the extra mile to get noticed by their racing heroes. Hard-core gearheads camp out days before a Piston Cup race to get the best view of their favorite racers as they speed by. Although most fans prefer to sit in the stands, rowdier attendees like to hang out at Redneck Hill in the center of the track—those cars know how to have a good time!

Fred truly is racing's number one fan. Some cars have better wax jobs or attached bumpers, but do they have the heart and dedication Fred has? Not a chance. Between Fred's racing blog, podcast, website, and daily call-ins to numerous radio shows, it's amazing he has time to get to any actual races.

VEHICLE TYPE:
Stodgey Suaver LT

FRED

MIA AND TIA

Mia and Tia haven't missed a race in over a year, but they'd be the first to tell you that they are not race fans but Lightning McQueen fans! Painted in his signature red and covered in Lightning McQueen stickers, the girls scream like crazy when their hero races. They scream like crazy when he poses for photos. And they scream like crazy all the way home just thinking about him.

VEHICLE TYPE:
1992 Mazda Miata

TIMOTHY TwoStroke

You will find no bigger Lightning McQueen fan than Timothy TwoStroke. He drove from New Jersey to California in just four days to see his favorite car in the legendary race! At the speed he was driving, Timothy shouldn't have been watching the race—he should have been in it.

VEHICLE TYPE:
Emerycraft

Sometimes Kit Revster can be found waxing and renting surfboards at the beach. More often he can be found closing shop early and hitting the waves. But not today. This morning Kit closed his surf shop for something truly special—the biggest race of the decade at the Los Angeles International Speedway.

VEHICLE TYPE:
Hollismobile Driftwood

KIT REVSTER

POLLY PUDDLEJUMPER

A mild-mannered homemaker by day, Polly Puddlejumper has rooted for The King ever since he blew past her on the outskirts of Placerville one summer afternoon in 1989. No one knows about her secret crush—and she plans to keep it that way!

VEHICLE TYPE:
Emerycraft

Matthew "True Blue" McCrew has been a fan of The King since he first came off the production line. In fact, everything in Matthew's house is painted King blue, including the lightbulbs. Because for Matthew, being a fan of The King isn't just reserved for race day, it's a way of life.

VEHICLE TYPE:
Brawny Motor Co. Leeway GT

MATTHEW "TRUE BLUE" McCREW

SYD VanDerKamper

Each year, Syd VanDerKamper migrates cross-country to see his favorite Piston Cup races. Last year, on his way to the Los Angeles International Speedway, he swung through Kingman, Arizona, where he found plastic flamingos at a local garage sale! Now a permanent fixture on Syd's "front lawn," his plastic bird friends have earned him an honored spot atop fabled Redneck Hill!

VEHICLE TYPE:
1986 Cloud Chaser RV

Albert Hinkey is not only Lightning McQueen's biggest fan. Known as Buffet Master among friends, Al can also guzzle two gas stations worth of fuel in one sitting! Al is the biggest and best friend anyone could ever have.

VEHICLE TYPE:
1985 Boxomatic Travel'bout 4XL

ALBERT HINKEY

R.M.

R.M. and Larry are the best of friends: these two can usually be found making trouble and takin' names on Redneck Hill. But despite their rowdy nature, they are true southern gentlemen and dead serious when it comes to racing.

VEHICLE TYPE:
1980 Boxomatic Coach 5.0 L V-8 Motor

Larry and R.M. know the stats on every team, which is useful since they always have a bet riding on who will be the next Piston Cup champion.

VEHICLE TYPE:
1980 Silverliner Coach 5.1 L V-8 Motor

LARRY

BARRY DIESEL

Barry loves Dinoco oil. He starts his day off with Dinoco's Extreme Octane, to give him that extra kick in the bumper, and then it's gallon after gallon of Dinoco regular to keep him running smooth all day. However, his wife thinks it's about time Barry switched to Dinoco Light.

VEHICLE TYPE:
1975 Silverliner Coach V-8

Clayton grew up in an RV park on the Monterey coast. He's a traveler by nature, so touring with his favorite races fits his lifestyle beautifully. He doesn't see himself ever settling down in one spot, not for longer than a weekend anyway. He just can't ignore the call of the open road.

VEHICLE TYPE:
Silverliner Drifter

CLAYTON GENTLEBREEZE

When Johnny and Jamie were young they spent more time goofing off at races than watching them. They've matured a bit since then and now know that it's silly to waste race time playing pranks and getting into trouble. That's why they now show up early to play pranks and get into trouble.

VEHICLE TYPE:
Nemomatic Menv

The Convoy Brothers have never been apart. They do absolutely everything together. They work together, have lunch together—they even have vacation sites next to each other. To see them you'd think they were welded at the fenders, but they're not . . . not anymore, thanks to the miracle of modern engineering.

VEHICLE TYPE:
Various Silverliner Makes

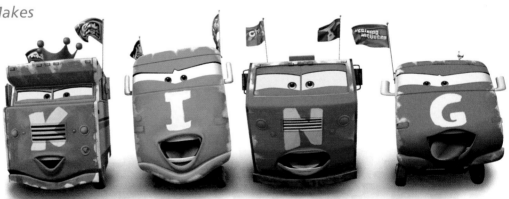

CONVOY BROTHERS

Young Coriander Widetrack has no interest in racing; her eyes are on the skies. While the other cars in school race around the playground pretending to be Lightning McQueen, Coriander turns that blacktop into blue sky, imagining she's soaring 10,000 feet in the air and racing to exotic destinations. It's Coriander's dream to someday meet one of her idols—a jet fighter.

VEHICLE TYPE:
Capitol Motors

Do fans have fans? Well Lightning McQueen's two superfans, Mia and Tia, do. Wilmar Flattz met Mia and Tia at a Lightning McQueen fan-club event last season, and he's been smitten ever since. Once, Wilmar actually gathered up the nerve to ask Tia what time it was. Her answer, "Quarter to three, I think," is a sweet, treasured memory he plays over and over in his head.

VEHICLE TYPE:
2000 Clebert Sniffler

WILMAR FLATTZ

MARTY BRAKEBURST

Marty doesn't feel alive unless he's got something to worry about. Whether it's his receding tire treads, politics, the teenagers next door, fossil fuel running out one day, or the general state of the world, Marty is only truly happy when he's miserable.

VEHICLE TYPE:
Remirunabout Neuro

Benny Brakedrum had never been to a race before—that is, until he was caller #7 on his favorite radio show, *Mornings with Eddy and the Dump Truck.* And just like that, he had two front-row tickets to the biggest event of the decade, as long as he wore his free Eddy and the Dump Truck bumper sticker!

VEHICLE TYPE:
Clebert Scooner

BENNY BRAKEDRUM

ALPHABETICAL INDEX OF CHARACTERS